MW00860694

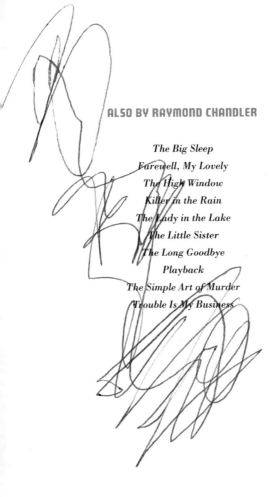

ALSO BY RAYMOND CHANDLER

Philip Marlowe's Guide to Life

Stephen -
12/25/05
Every man needs a
good line handy -
unless they look
like you . . .

Ketzel ♡

PHILIP MARLOWE'S GUIDE TO LIFE

A Compendium of Quotations by

RAYMOND CHANDLER

Edited by Martin Asher

Alfred A. Knopf · New York · 2005

THIS IS A BORZOI BOOK
PUBLISHED BY ALFRED A. KNOPF

Published in the United States by Alfred A. Knopf, a division of
Random House, Inc., New York, and in Canada by Random
House of Canada Limited, Toronto.

www.aaknopf.com

Knopf, Borzoi Books, and the colophon are registered
trademarks of Random House, Inc.

Library of Congress Cataloging-in-Publication Data
Chandler, Raymond, 1888–1959.
  Philip Marlowe's guide to life / by Raymond Chandler ; edited
by Martin Asher.
    p. cm.
  ISBN: 1-4000-4158-9
  1. Chandler, Raymond, 1888–1959—Quotations. 2. Marlowe,
Philip (Fictitious character) I. Asher, Marty. II. Title.
PS3505.H3224A6 2005
813'.52—dc22   2005013866

Manufactured in the United States of America
First Edition

Acknowledgments: The editor wishes to thank Edward Kasten-
meier, Victoria Skurnick, Eric Martinez, Jordan Pavlin, Joe
Spieler, and Margaux Wexberg for their invaluable assistance;
and Sonny Mehta and Ed Victor for their support.

INTRODUCTION

I have always been a fan of Raymond Chandler's for many reasons, not the least of which is that he is a stylist whose best one-liners can rival Shakespeare's, or at least Oscar Wilde's. From the classic "a blonde to make a bishop kick a hole in a stained glass window," to "in Hollywood anything can happen, anything at all," Chandler is unquestionably a virtuoso who can pin down in a sentence what would take lesser writers paragraphs. But upon rereading Chandler's work recently, I noticed something else, something more substantial, which transforms Chandler from a mere "stylist" into one of the great writers of his time. His work, and in particular the vision of his main character and alter ego, Philip Marlowe, offers a moral code even more valuable and relevant now than it was almost three-quarters of a century ago when Chandler wrote it.

Marlowe was both smart and cool. In a world that had just seen the rise of the most barbaric regimes in history, he was sensitive enough to know right from wrong but tough enough to knock you around if you even thought about doing anything sleazy. Whether he was writing about women ("they say lust makes a man old, but keeps a woman young") or cops ("he was the kind of cop who spits on his blackjack every night instead of saying his prayers"), Marlowe had a way of seeing the world as a place where evil was rampant and needed to be aggressively sought out and eradicated. As his books progressed, even Los Angeles itself, previously portrayed by most writers in loving pastels, became a sinister terrain where palm trees hovered menacingly over filthy two-bit downtown hotels reeking with treachery and murder ("It was night. The world outside the windows was a black world").

Raymond Chandler started out thinking he was writing private-eye pulp. From 1933 on, he wrote stories for magazines with names like *Black Mask* and *Detective Fiction Weekly*. But with the publication of *The Big Sleep* in 1939, by the tony house of Knopf (all right, a cheap plug Marlowe never would have approved of), Chandler took a quantum leap forward and from the clichés of the genre breathed life into one of the most popular and original characters in twentieth-century American fiction. His protagonist, Philip Marlowe, while maintaining all the external trappings of the detective genre—the raincoat, the fedora, the tough-guy attitude—was really a man who had as much in common with Don Quixote as he did with Sam Spade. Marlowe was an unending crusader for justice, whether investigating a dying, eccentric millionaire whose troublesome daughters are being blackmailed (*The Big Sleep*) or trying to save a friend whom everyone else seems to have abandoned (*The Long Goodbye*).

As John Bayley notes in his introduction to the collected stories, "Unlike his many predecessors, Philip Marlowe is a lone wolf, a single operator working on his own 'down mean streets' as Chandler was to put it, in his wry, cynical, understated endeavor not only to find out the truth but to make justice prevail in a corrupt world, a world which neither knows nor cares for the meaning of the word."

But while evil was a problem in Marlowe's time, at least if you had enough smarts, you could figure out who were the good guys and who were the bad guys (women could be bad guys, too). But what, I wonder, would Marlowe have made of Richard Nixon? Of Kenneth Lay? Or Martha Stewart (not exactly Marlowe's kind of blonde). Not to mention Rush Limbaugh, Michael Jackson, Donald Trump, Madonna, or George Steinbrenner. I have therefore assembled some of the great one-liners and observations of Marlowe in a concise format for easy reference in these troubled times. I've arranged the subjects alphabetically, which shows the surprising breadth of his vision (I was *not* expecting to find references to T. S. Eliot and Chopin) and might also come in handy should a reader walk into a room, find a naked woman on a bed, and need a quick response: "I appreciate all you're offering me. It's just more than I could possibly take."

This little book is by no means intended to be a comprehensive collection of Chandler quotations, but rather an attempt to re-create the outlines of Marlowe's message and style for a generation that needs it more than ever. But maybe even that's asking too much. It's probably enough just to hope that it might serve as an introduction for the uninitiated to one of the most profoundly original and obscenely enjoyable writers America has ever produced.

—Martin Asher

Philip Marlowe's Guide to Life

ADVERTISING

As elaborate a waste of human
intelligence as you could find
anywhere outside an advertising
agency.

The Long Goodbye

The commercials would have sickened
a goat raised on barbed wire and
broken beer bottles.

The Long Goodbye

ARCHITECTURE

Maybe this idiotic hunk of
architecture depressed her. It would
have depressed a laughing jackass
and made it coo like a mourning dove.

The Long Goodbye

The house itself was not so much. It was smaller than Buckingham Palace, rather gray for California, and probably had fewer windows than the Chrysler Building.

Farewell, My Lovely

There were all sorts of ornamental trees in clumps here and there and they didn't look like California trees. Imported stuff. Whoever built that place was trying to drag the Atlantic seaboard over the Rockies. He was trying hard, but he hadn't made it.

The Long Goodbye

Montemar Vista was a few dozen houses of various sizes and shapes

hanging by their teeth and eyebrows
to a spur of mountain and looking as
if a good sneeze would drop them down
among the box lunches on the beach.

Farewell, My Lovely

About the only part of a California
house you can't put your foot through
is the front door.

The Big Sleep

BIG MEN

He was a large man and wide. Not
young nor handsome, but he looked
durable. Above the sky-blue
gabardine slacks he wore a two-tone
leisure jacket which would have been
revolting on a zebra. The neck of his

5

canary-yellow shirt was open wide,
which it had to be if his neck was
going to get out.

The Little Sister

BLONDES

There is the soft and willing and
alcoholic blonde who doesn't care
what she wears as long as it is mink
or where she goes as long as it is the
Starlight Roof and there is plenty of
dry champagne. There is the small
perky blonde who is a little pal and
wants to pay her own way and is full
of sunshine and common sense and
knows judo from the ground up and
can toss a truck driver over her
shoulder without missing more than
one sentence out of the editorial in
the *Saturday Review.* There is the
pale, pale blonde with anemia of some
non-fatal but incurable type. She is
very languid and very shadowy and

she speaks softly out of nowhere and
you can't lay a finger on her because
in the first place you don't want to
and in the second place she is
reading *The Waste Land* or Dante in
the original, or Kafka or Kierkegaard
or studying Provençal. She adores
music and when the New York
Philharmonic is playing Hindemith
she can tell you which one of the six
bass viols came in a quarter of a beat
too late. I hear Toscanini can also.
That makes two of them.

The Long Goodbye

It was a blonde. A blonde to make a
bishop kick a hole in a stained glass
window.

Farewell, My Lovely

BOOZE

"Alcohol is like love," he said. "The
first kiss is magic, the second is
intimate, the third is routine. After
that you take the girl's clothes off."

The Long Goodbye

"I like the neat bottles on the bar
back and the lovely shining glasses
and the anticipation. I like to watch
the man mix the first one of the
evening and put it down on a crisp
mat and put the little folded napkin
beside it. I like to taste it slowly.
The first quiet drink of the evening
in a quiet bar—that's wonderful."

The Long Goodbye

There was a sad fellow over on a bar
stool talking to the bartender, who
was polishing a glass and listening

with that plastic smile people wear
when they are trying not to scream.

The Long Goodbye

It was the same old cocktail party,
everybody talking too loud, nobody
listening, everybody hanging on for
dear life to a mug of the juice, eyes
very bright, cheeks flushed or pale or
sweaty according to the amount of
alcohol consumed and the capacity of
the individual to handle it.

The Long Goodbye

"I don't drink. The more I see of
people who do, the more glad I am that
I don't."

The Long Goodbye

That was that. We said good-bye and hung up. The coffee shop smell from next door came in at the windows with the soot but failed to make me hungry. So I got out my office bottle and took the drink and let my self-respect ride its own race.

The Big Sleep

The whiskey had a funny taste. While I was realizing that it had a funny taste I saw a washbowl jammed into the corner of the wall. I made it. I just made it. I vomited. Dizzy Dean never threw anything harder.

Farewell, My Lovely

"You know, you'll have to taste water sometime, just for the hell of it." She came over and took my glass. "This is going to be the last."

Farewell, My Lovely

The fog had cleared off outside and the stars were as bright as artificial stars of chromium on a sky of black velvet. I drove fast. I needed a drink badly and the bars were closed.

Farewell, My Lovely

BRASS KNUCKLES

"If you're big enough you don't need them, and if you need them you're not big enough to push me around."

The Long Goodbye

It was a nice face, a face you get to like. Pretty, but not so pretty that you would have to wear brass knuckles every time you took it out.

Farewell, My Lovely

CAPITAL PUNISHMENT

"Keep quiet or you'll get the same and more of it. Just lie quiet and hold your breath. Hold it until you can't hold it any longer and then tell yourself that you have to breathe, that you're black in the face, that your eyeballs are popping out, and that you're going to breathe right now, but that you're sitting strapped in the chair in the clean little gas chamber up in San Quentin and when you take that breath you're fighting with all your soul not to take it, it won't be air you'll get, it will be cyanide fumes. And that's what they call humane execution in our state now."

The Big Sleep

CHESS

I looked down at the chessboard. The move with the knight was wrong. I put

it back where I had moved it from.
Knights had no meaning in this game.
It wasn't a game for knights.

The Big Sleep

CHOPIN

The boss mortician fluttered around
making elegant little gestures and
body movements as graceful as a
Chopin ending.

The Little Sister

CHRISTMAS

I knocked the cold ashes out of my
pipe and refilled it from the leather
humidor an admirer had given me for
Christmas, the admirer by an odd

coincidence having the same name as
mine.

The Little Sister

The stores along Hollywood Boulevard
were already beginning to fill up
with overpriced Christmas junk, and
the daily papers were beginning to
scream about how terrible it would be
if you didn't get your Christmas
shopping done early. It would be
terrible anyway; it always is.

The Long Goodbye

CIGARETTES

My stomach burned from the last
drink. I wasn't hungry. I lit a
cigarette. It tasted like a plumber's
handkerchief.

Farewell, My Lovely

"You may smoke, sir. I like the smell of tobacco."

I lit the cigarette and blew a lungful at him and he sniffed at it like a terrier at a rathole. The faint smile pulled at the shadowed corners of his mouth.

The Big Sleep

I puffed at the cigarette. It was one of those things with filters in them. It tasted like a high fog strained through cotton wool.

The Long Goodbye

CITIES

I would have stayed in the town where I was born and worked in the hardware store and married the boss's daughter and had five kids and read them the funny paper on Sunday

morning and smacked their heads when
they got out of line and squabbled
with the wife about how much spending
money they were to get and what
programs they could have on the radio
or TV set. I might even have got rich—
small-town rich, an eight-room house,
two cars in the garage, chicken every
Sunday and the *Reader's Digest* on the
living room table, the wife with a
cast-iron permanent and me with a
brain like a sack of Portland cement.
You take it, friend. I'll take the big
sordid dirty crowded city.

The Long Goodbye

"Sure, it's a nice town. It's probably
no crookeder than Los Angeles. But
you can only buy a piece of a big city.
You can buy a town this size all
complete, with the original box and
tissue paper. That's the difference.
And that makes me want out."

Farewell, My Lovely

COFFEE

I drank two cups black. Then I tried a
cigarette. It was all right. I still
belonged to the human race.

The Long Goodbye

I went out to the kitchen to make
coffee—yards of coffee. Rich, strong,
bitter, boiling hot, ruthless,
depraved. The life-blood of tired
men.

The Long Goodbye

COLORFUL MEN

A male cutie with henna'd hair
drooped at a bungalow grand piano
and tickled the keys lasciviously and

17

sang "Stairway to the Stars" in a
voice with half the steps missing.

Farewell, My Lovely

The fellow who decorated that room
was not a man to let colors scare him.
He probably wore a pimiento shirt,
mulberry slacks, zebra shoes, and
vermilion drawers with his initials
on them in a nice Mandarin orange.

The Long Goodbye

"He was like Caesar, a husband to
women and a wife to men. Think I
can't figure people like him and you
out?"

The Big Sleep

COPS

An honest cop with a bad conscience
always acts tough. So does a
dishonest cop. So does almost anyone,
including me.

The Long Goodbye

"Cops get very large and emphatic
when an outsider tries to hide
anything, but they do the same things
themselves every other day, to oblige
their friends or anybody with a little
pull."

The Big Sleep

"In one way cops are all the same.
They all blame the wrong things. If a
guy loses his pay check at a crap
table, stop gambling. If he gets
drunk, stop liquor. If he kills

somebody in a car crash, stop making
automobiles. If he gets pinched with a
girl in a hotel room, stop sexual
intercourse. If he falls downstairs,
stop building houses."

The Long Goodbye

"Cops are just people," she said
irrelevantly.

"They start out that way, I've
heard."

Farewell, My Lovely

In our town the mobs don't kill a cop.
They leave that to the juveniles. And
a live cop who has been put through
the meat grinder is a much better
advertisement. He gets well
eventually and goes back to work. But
from that time on something is
missing—the last inch of steel that
makes all the difference. He's a

walking lesson that it is a mistake to push the racket boys too hard—especially if you are on the vice squad and eating at the best places and driving a Cadillac.

The Long Goodbye

"Cops are like a doctor that gives you aspirin for a brain tumor, except that the cop would rather cure it with a blackjack."

The Long Goodbye

He was the kind of cop who spits on his blackjack every night instead of saying his prayers.

Farewell, My Lovely

They had watching and waiting eyes, patient and careful eyes, cool disdainful eyes, cops' eyes. They get them at the passing-out parade at the police school.

The Long Goodbye

CRIME

"That's the difference between crime and business. For business you gotta have capital. Sometimes I think it's the only difference."

The Long Goodbye

Crime isn't a disease, it's a symptom.

The Long Goodbye

We're a big rough rich wild people and crime is the price we pay for it, and organized crime is the price we pay for organization.

The Long Goodbye

DAMES

"I like smooth shiny girls, hardboiled and loaded with sin."

Farewell, My Lovely

"I didn't ask to see you. You sent for me. I don't mind your ritzing me or drinking your lunch out of a Scotch bottle. I don't mind your showing me your legs. They're very swell legs and it's a pleasure to make their acquaintance. I don't mind if you don't like my manners. They're pretty bad. I grieve over them during long winter evenings."

The Big Sleep

To say she had a face that would have
stopped a clock would have been to
insult her. It would have stopped a
runaway horse.

The Little Sister

A slice of spumoni wouldn't have
melted on her now.

The Long Goodbye

Then she lowered her lashes until
they almost cuddled her cheeks and
slowly raised them again, like a
theater curtain. I was to get to know
that trick. That was supposed to make
me roll over on my back with all four
paws in the air.

The Big Sleep

I looked back as I opened the door.
Slim, dark and lovely and smiling.
Reeking with sex. Utterly beyond the
moral laws of this or any world I
could imagine.

She was one for the book all right.
I went out quietly. Very softly her
voice came to me as I closed the door.

"Querido—I have liked you very
much. It is too bad."

I shut the door.

The Little Sister

A pretty, spoiled and not very bright
little girl who had gone very, very
wrong, and nobody was doing anything
about it.

The Big Sleep

Her face under my mouth was like ice.
She put her hands up and took hold of

my head and kissed me hard on the
lips. Her lips were like ice, too.

I went out through the door and it
closed behind me, without sound, and
the rain blew in under the porch, not
as cold as her lips.

The Big Sleep

I left her laughing. The sound was
like a hen having hiccups.

Farewell, My Lovely

She came back with the glass and her
fingers cold from holding the cold
glass touched mine and I held them
for a moment and then let them go
slowly as you let go of a dream when
you wake with the sun in your face
and have been in an enchanted valley.

Farewell, My Lovely

You can have a hangover from other things than alcohol. I had one from women. Women made me sick.

The Big Sleep

DEATH

A dead man is the best fall guy in the world. He never talks back.

The Long Goodbye

Dead men are heavier than broken hearts.

The Big Sleep

The smell of sage drifted up from a canyon and made me think of a dead man and a moonless sky.

Farewell, My Lovely

What did it matter where you lay once
you were dead? In a dirty sump or in
a marble tower on top of a high hill?
You were dead, you were sleeping the
big sleep, you were not bothered by
things like that. Oil and water were
the same as wind and air to you. You
just slept the big sleep, not caring
about the nastiness of how you died
or where you fell.

The Big Sleep

"You mean something has happened to
him?" Her voice faded off into a sort
of sad whisper, like a mortician
asking for a down payment.

The Little Sister

"He's really dead?" she whispered.
"Really?"
   "He's dead," I said. "Dead, dead,
dead. Lady, he's dead."

Trouble Is My Business

DECORATING

It had the sort of lobby that asks for plush and india-rubber plants, but gets glass brick, cornice lighting, three-cornered glass tables, and a general air of having been redecorated by a parolee from a nut hatch. Its color scheme was bile green, linseed-poultice brown, sidewalk gray and monkey-bottom blue. It was as restful as a split lip.

The Little Sister

DIVORCE

"The first divorce is the only tough one. After that it's merely a problem in economics."

The Long Goodbye

DOCTORS

Doctors are just people, born to sorrow, fighting the long grim fight like the rest of us.

The Lady in the Lake

ELIOT, T. S.

" 'I grow old . . . I grow old . . . I shall wear the bottoms of my trousers rolled.' What does that mean, Mr. Marlowe?"

"Not a bloody thing. It just sounds good."

He smiled. "That is from the 'Love Song of J. Alfred Prufrock.' Here's another one. 'In the room the women come and go / Talking of Michael

Angelo.' Does that suggest anything to you, sir?"

"Yeah—it suggests to me that the guy didn't know very much about women."

The Long Goodbye

I went on out and Amos had the Caddy there waiting. He drove me back to Hollywood. I offered him a buck but he wouldn't take it. I offered to buy him the poems of T. S. Eliot. He said he already had them.

The Long Goodbye

EXPENSIVE PERFUME

It was definitely the stuff to get. One drop of that in the hollow of your

throat and the matched pink pearls
started falling on you like summer
rain.

The Lady in the Lake

EYES

His eyes were deep like that. And they
were also eyes without expression,
without soul, eyes that could watch
lions tear a man to pieces and never
change, that could watch a man
impaled and screaming in the hot sun
with his eyelids cut off.

Farewell, My Lovely

They had the eyes they always have,
cloudy and gray like freezing water.
The firm set mouth, the hard little
wrinkles at the corners of the eyes,
the hard hollow meaningless stare,

not quite cruel and a thousand miles
from kind.

The Little Sister

FACES

It was a face that had nothing to
fear. Everything had been done to it
that anybody could think of.

Farewell, My Lovely

FAST LIVING

I got up and went to the built-in
wardrobe and looked at my face in the
flawed mirror. It was me all right. I
had a strained look. I'd been living
too fast.

The Little Sister

FOOD

Americans will eat anything if it is
toasted and held together with a
couple of toothpicks and has lettuce
sticking out of the sides, preferably
a little wilted.

The Long Goodbye

"You've got enough shady friends to
know different."
    "They're all soft compared to you."
    "Thanks, lady. You're no English
muffin yourself."

The Big Sleep

Down at the drugstore lunch counter I
had time to inhale two cups of coffee
and a melted-cheese sandwich with

two slivers of ersatz bacon imbedded
in it, like dead fish in the silt at the
bottom of a drained pool.

The Little Sister

The eighty-five-cent dinner tasted
like a discarded mail bag and was
served to me by a waiter who looked
as if he would slug me for a quarter,
cut my throat for six bits, and bury
me at sea in a barrel of concrete for
a dollar and a half, plus sales tax.

Farewell, My Lovely

GRAMMAR

"He coulda went somewhere without
telling me," he mused.

"Your grammar," I said, "is almost
as loose as your toupee."

The Little Sister

HEMINGWAY

"Who is this Hemingway person at
all?"

"A guy that keeps saying the same
thing over and over until you begin
to believe it must be good."

Farewell, My Lovely

HOLLYWOOD

In Hollywood anything can happen,
anything at all.

The Long Goodbye

HOME

I didn't mind what she called me, what
anybody called me. But this was the
room I had to live in. It was all I had
in the way of a home. In it was
everything that was mine, that had

any association for me, any past,
anything that took the place of a
family. Not much; a few books,
pictures, radio, chessmen, old letters,
stuff like that. Nothing. Such as they
were they had all my memories.

The Big Sleep

I unlocked the door of my apartment
and went in and sniffed the smell of
it, just standing there, against the
door for a little while before I put
the light on. A homely smell, a smell
of dust and tobacco smoke, the smell
of a world where men live, and keep on
living.

Farewell, My Lovely

INSECTS

Mr. Lindsay Marriott's face looked as if he had swallowed a bee. He smoothed it out with an effort.

"You have a somewhat peculiar sense of humor," he said.

"Not peculiar," I said. "Just uninhibited."

Farewell, My Lovely

His long fingers made movements like dying butterflies.

Farewell, My Lovely

A dead moth was spread-eagled on a corner of the desk. On the window sill a bee with tattered wings was crawling along the woodwork, buzzing

in a tired remote sort of way, as if
she knew it wasn't any use, she was
finished, she had flown too many
missions and would never get back to
the hive again.

The Long Goodbye

"If I had a razor, I'd cut your
throat—just to see what ran out
of it."

"Caterpillar blood," I said.

The Big Sleep

JAIL

In jail a man has no personality. He
is a minor disposal problem and a few
entries on reports. Nobody cares who
loves or hates him, what he looks like,
what he did with his life. Nobody
reacts to him unless he gives trouble.
Nobody abuses him. All that is asked

of him is that he go quietly to the
right cell and remain quiet when he
gets there.

The Long Goodbye

KHACHATURYAN VIOLIN CONCERTO

At three A.M. I was walking the floor
and listening to Khachaturyan
working in a tractor factory. He
called it a violin concerto. I called
it a loose fan belt and the hell
with it.

The Long Goodbye

KISSES

"A kiss doesn't seem to mean much
nowadays."

The Long Goodbye

KITTENS

I grinned at her. The little blonde at
the **PBX** cocked a shell-like ear and
smiled a small fluffy smile. She
looked playful and eager, but not
quite sure of herself, like a new
kitten in a house where they don't
care much about kittens.

The Lady in the Lake

She kind of held the purse so I could
see how empty it was. Then she
straightened the bills out on the desk
and put one on top of the other and
pushed them across. Very slowly, very
sadly, as if she was drowning a
favorite kitten.

The Little Sister

LAS VEGAS

"He's on a bus going to Las Vegas. He has a friend there who will give him a job."

She brightened up very suddenly. "Oh—to Las Vegas? How sentimental of him. That's where we were married."

"I guess he forgot," I said, "or he would have gone somewhere else."

The Long Goodbye

LAW

"The law isn't justice. It's a very imperfect mechanism. If you press exactly the right buttons and are also lucky, justice may show up in the answer."

The Long Goodbye

LIARS

For a moment I almost believed him.
His face was as smooth as an angel's
wing.

Farewell, My Lovely

LITERATURE

He was a guy who talked with commas,
like a heavy novel.

The Long Goodbye

LONELINESS

Room 332 was at the back of the
building near the door to the fire
escape. The corridor which led to it
had a smell of old carpet and
furniture oil and the drab anonymity
of a thousand shabby lives.

The Little Sister

Lonely men always talk too much.
Either that or they don't talk at all.

The Little Sister

I was as hollow and empty as the
spaces between the stars.

The Long Goodbye

I was as empty of life as a
scarecrow's pockets.

The Big Sleep

LOS ANGELES

There were two hundred and eighty
steps up to Cabrillo Street. They were
drifted over with windblown sand and
the handrail was as cold and wet as a
toad's belly.

Farewell, My Lovely

After a while there was a faint smell
of ocean. Not very much, but as if
they had kept this much just to
remind people this had once been a
clean open beach where the waves
came in and creamed and the wind
blew and you could smell something
besides hot fat and cold sweat.

Farewell, My Lovely

On the right the great fat solid
Pacific trudging into shore like a
scrubwoman going home. No moon, no
fuss, hardly a sound of the surf. No
smell. None of the harsh wild smell of
the sea. A California ocean.

The Little Sister

"Los Angeles was just a big dry sunny
place with ugly homes and no style,
but goodhearted and peaceful. It had
the climate they just yap about now.

People used to sleep out on porches.
Little groups who thought they were
intellectual used to call it the
Athens of America. It wasn't that, but
it wasn't a neon-lighted slum either."

The Little Sister

When I got home I mixed a stiff one
and stood by the open window in the
living room and sipped it and
listened to the groundswell of the
traffic on Laurel Canyon Boulevard
and looked at the glare of the big
angry city hanging over the shoulder
of the hills through which the
boulevard had been cut. Far off the
banshee wail of police or fire sirens
rose and fell, never for very long
completely silent. Twenty-four hours
a day somebody is running, somebody
else is trying to catch him. Out there

in the night of a thousand crimes
people were dying, being maimed, cut
by flying glass, crushed against
steering wheels or under heavy tires.
People were being beaten, robbed,
strangled, raped, and murdered.
People were hungry, sick, bored,
desperate with loneliness or remorse
or fear, angry, cruel, feverish, shaken
by sobs. A city no worse than others,
a city rich and vigorous and full of
pride, a city lost and beaten and full
of emptiness.

The Long Goodbye

LOVE

"Love is such a dull word," she mused.
"It amazes me that the English
language so rich in the poetry of love
can accept such a feeble word for it.
It has no life, no resonance. It
suggests to me little girls in ruffled
summer dresses, with little pink

smiles, and little shy voices, and probably the most unbecoming underwear."

The Little Sister

LUXURY CARS

It moved away from the curb and around the corner with as much noise as a bill makes in a wallet.

Trouble Is My Business

MARLOWE, PHILIP

"Tell me a little about yourself, Mr. Marlowe. That is, if you don't find the request objectionable."

"What sort of thing? I'm a licensed private investigator and have been for quite a while. I'm a lone wolf, unmarried, getting middle-aged, and not rich. I've been in jail more than once and I don't do divorce business.

I like liquor and women and chess and a few other things. The cops don't like me too well, but I know a couple I get along with. I'm a native son, born in Santa Rosa, both parents dead, no brothers or sisters, and when I get knocked off in a dark alley sometime, if it happens, as it could to anyone in my business, and to plenty of people in any business or no business at all these days, nobody will feel that the bottom has dropped out of his or her life."

The Long Goodbye

MARLOWE, PHIL

"You're as cold-blooded a beast as I ever met, Marlowe. Or can I call you Phil?"

"Sure."

"You can call me Vivian."

"Thanks, Mrs. Regan."

"Oh, go to hell, Marlowe."

The Big Sleep

MARRIAGE

"For two people in a hundred it's wonderful."

The Long Goodbye

His surprise was as thin as the gold on a weekend wedding ring.

The Long Goodbye

"But you know how it is with marriage—any marriage. After a while a guy like me, a common no-good guy like me, he wants to feel a leg. Some

other leg. Maybe it's lousy, but that's
the way it is."

The Lady in the Lake

MONEY

"Big money is big power and big power
gets used wrong. It's the system.
Maybe it's the best we can get, but it
still ain't any Ivory Soap deal."

The Long Goodbye

MORNING

Next morning I got up late on account
of the big fee I had earned the night
before. I drank an extra cup of
coffee, smoked an extra cigarette, ate
an extra slice of Canadian bacon, and
for the three hundredth time I swore I
would never again use an electric
razor.

The Long Goodbye

I was sitting on the side of my bed in
my pajamas, thinking about getting
up, but not yet committed. I didn't
feel very well, but I didn't feel as
sick as I ought to, not as sick as I
would feel if I had a salaried job.

Farewell, My Lovely

My head hurt and felt large and hot
and my tongue was dry and had gravel
on it and my throat was stiff and my
jaw was not untender. But I had had
worse mornings.

Farewell, My Lovely

It was a crisp morning, with just
enough snap in the air to make life

seem simple and sweet, if you didn't
have too much on your mind. I did.

The Big Sleep

Then her hands dropped and jerked at
something and the robe she was
wearing came open and underneath it
she was naked as a September Morn
but a darn sight less coy.

The Long Goodbye

NEEDS

I needed a drink, I needed a lot of
life insurance, I needed a vacation, I
needed a home in the country. What I
had was a coat, a hat and a gun.

Farewell, My Lovely

NIGHT

It was night. The world outside the
windows was a black world.

Farewell, My Lovely

NOTHING

After that nothing happened for three
days. Nobody slugged me or shot at me
or called me up on the phone and
warned me to keep my nose clean.
Nobody hired me to find the
wandering daughter, the erring wife,
the lost pearl necklace, or the
missing will. I just sat there and
looked at the wall.

The Long Goodbye

"Men have been shot for practically
nothing."

The Big Sleep

ORCHIDS

The plants filled the place, a forest
of them, with nasty meaty leaves and
stalks like the newly washed fingers
of dead men. They smelled as
overpowering as boiling alcohol
under a blanket.

The Big Sleep

"They are nasty things. Their flesh is
too much like the flesh of men. And
their perfume has the rotten
sweetness of a prostitute."

The Big Sleep

PEKINESE

I stepped past the crawling girl and picked the gun up. She looked up at me and began to giggle. I put her gun in my pocket and patted her on the back. "Get up, angel. You look like a Pekinese."

The Big Sleep

POLITICS

Sheriff Petersen just went right on getting re-elected, a living testimonial to the fact that you can hold an important public office forever in our country with no qualifications for it but a clean nose, a photogenic face, and a closed mouth. If on top of that you look good on a horse, you are unbeatable.

The Long Goodbye

"It would take more than a private dick to bother me," he said.

"No, it wouldn't. A private dick can bother anybody. He's persistent and used to snubs. He's paid for his time and he would just as soon use it to bother you as any other way."

The Lady in the Lake

"The first time we met I told you I was a detective. Get it through your lovely head. I work at it, lady. I don't play at it."

The Big Sleep

"Just what do you want done, Mr. Kingsley?"

"What do you care? You do all kinds of detective work, don't you?"

"Not all kinds. Only the fairly honest kinds."

The Lady in the Lake

"I don't think I'd care to employ a detective that uses liquor in any form. I don't even approve of tobacco."

"Would it be all right if I peeled an orange?"

I caught the sharp intake of breath at the far end of the line. "You might at least talk like a gentleman," she said.

"Better try the University Club," I told her. "I heard they had a couple left over there, but I'm not sure they'll let you handle them." I hung up.

The Little Sister

"I understand you are a private detective?"

"Yes."

"I think you are a very stupid person. You look stupid. You are in a stupid business. And you came here on a stupid mission."

"I get it," I said. "I'm stupid. It sank in after a while."

Farewell, My Lovely

So passed a day in the life of a P.I. Not exactly a typical day but not totally untypical either. What makes a man stay with it nobody knows. You don't get rich, you don't often have much fun. Sometimes you get beaten up or shot at or tossed into the jailhouse. Once in a long while you get dead. Every other month you

decide to give it up and find some
sensible occupation while you can
still walk without shaking your head.
Then the door buzzer rings and you
open the inner door to the waiting
room and there stands a new face with
a new problem, a new load of grief,
and a small piece of money.

The Long Goodbye

PROUST, MARCEL

"I was beginning to think perhaps you
worked in bed, like Marcel Proust."

"Who's he?" I put a cigarette in my
mouth and stared at her. She looked a
little pale and strained, but she
looked like a girl who could function
under a strain.

"A French writer, a connoisseur in
degenerates. You wouldn't know him."

"Tut, tut," I said. "Come into my
boudoir."

The Big Sleep

PUBLISHERS

"You're at a cocktail party and get introduced to all sorts of people, and some of them have novels written and you are just liquored up enough to be benevolent and full of love for the human race, so you say you'd love to see the script. It is then dropped at your hotel with such sickening speed that you are forced to go through the motions of reading it."

The Long Goodbye

THE RICH

He was about as hard to see as the Dalai Lama. Guys with a hundred million dollars live a peculiar life, behind a screen of servants, bodyguards, secretaries, lawyers, and tame executives. Presumably they eat, sleep, get their hair cut, and wear clothes. But you never know for sure.

Everything you read or hear about them has been processed by a public relations gang of guys who are paid big money to create and maintain a usable personality, something simple and clean and sharp, like a sterilized needle. It doesn't have to be true. It just has to be consistent with the known facts, and the known facts you could count on your fingers.

The Long Goodbye

They say the rich can always protect themselves and that in their world it is always summer. I've lived with them and they are bored and lonely people.

The Long Goodbye

"Well?" she asked me quietly. "How did you get on with Father?"

"Fine. He explained civilization to

me. I mean how it looks to him. He's going to let it go on for a little while longer. But it better be careful and not interfere with his private life. If it does, he's apt to make a phone call to God and cancel the order."

The Long Goodbye

"They never want anything very hard except maybe somebody else's wife and that's a pretty pale desire compared with the way a plumber's wife wants new curtains for the living room."

The Long Goodbye

"I'm rich. Who the hell wants to be happy?"

The Long Goodbye

ROLLS-ROYCE

Her hair was a lovely shade of dark
red and she had a distant smile on
her lips and over her shoulders
she had a blue mink that almost made
the Rolls-Royce look like just
another automobile. It didn't quite.
Nothing can.

The Long Goodbye

SANTA ANA WINDS

There was a desert wind blowing that
night. It was one of those hot dry
Santa Anas that come down through
the mountain passes and curl your
hair and make your nerves jump and
your skin itch. On nights like that

every booze party ends in a fight.
Meek little wives feel the edge of the
carving knife and study their
husbands' necks.

Trouble Is My Business

Everywhere along the way gardens
were full of withered and blackened
leaves and flowers which the hot wind
had burned.

Trouble Is My Business

SCOTCH

The swift California twilight was
falling. It was a lovely night. Venus
in the west was as bright as a street
lamp, as bright as life, as bright as
Miss Huntress' eyes, as bright as a
bottle of Scotch.

Trouble Is My Business

The Scotch, as good enough Scotch
will, stayed with me all the way back
to Hollywood. I took the red lights as
they came.

Farewell, My Lovely

On the way down in the elevator I had
an impulse to go back up and take the
Scotch bottle away from him. But it
wasn't any of my business and it
never does any good anyway. They
always find a way to get it if they
have to have it.

The Long Goodbye

SEX

"It's excitement of a high order, but
it's an impure emotion—impure in the
aesthetic sense. I'm not sneering at
sex. It's necessary and it doesn't
have to be ugly. But it always has to

be managed. Making it glamorous is a billion-dollar industry and it costs every cent of it."

The Long Goodbye

The imprint of her head was still in the pillow, of her small corrupt body still on the sheets. I put my empty glass down and tore the bed to pieces savagely.

The Big Sleep

They say lust makes a man old, but keeps a woman young. They say a lot of nonsense.

The Long Goodbye

She sighed. "All men are the same."

   "So are all women—after the first
nine."

Farewell, My Lovely

The purring voice was now as false as
an usherette's eyelashes and as
slippery as a watermelon seed.

The Big Sleep

SMILES

Her smile was cozy and acid at the
same time.

Farewell, My Lovely

His smile was as stiff as a frozen
fish.

Farewell, My Lovely

She had an iron smile and eyes that could count the money in your hip wallet.

The Long Goodbye

The sunshine was as empty as a headwaiter's smile.

The Big Sleep

SMOG

Everything was the fault of the smog. If the canary wouldn't sing, if the milkman was late, if the Pekinese had fleas, if an old coot in a starched collar had a heart attack on the way to church, that was the smog.

The Long Goodbye

SOCIETY

But otherwise he looked like any other nice young guy in a dinner jacket who had been spending too much money in a joint that exists for that purpose and for no other.

The Long Goodbye

SORE KNUCKLES

His chin came down and I hit it. I hit it as if I was driving the last spike on the first transcontinental railroad. I can still feel it when I flex my knuckles.

Trouble Is My Business

SPARROWS

Live oaks clustered towards the road,
as if they were curious to see who
went by, and sparrows with rosy
heads hopped about pecking at things
only a sparrow would think worth
pecking at.

The Long Goodbye

SUBURBAN LIFE

A club owned the lake and the lake
frontage and if they didn't want you
in the club, you didn't get to play in
the water. It was exclusive in the
only remaining sense of the word that
doesn't mean merely expensive.

I belonged in Idle Valley like a
pearl onion on a banana split.

The Long Goodbye

It was going to be hot later, but in a
nice refined exclusive sort of way,

nothing brutal like the heat of the desert, not sticky and rank like the heat of the city. Idle Valley was a perfect place to live. Perfect. Nice people with nice homes, nice cars, nice horses, nice dogs, possibly even nice children.

But all a man named Marlowe wanted from it was out. And fast.

The Long Goodbye

SUICIDES

Suicides prepare themselves in all sorts of ways, some with liquor, some with elaborate champagne dinners. Some in evening clothes, some in no clothes. People have killed themselves on the tops of walls, in ditches, in bathrooms, in the water, over the water, on the water. They have hanged themselves in bars and gassed themselves in garages. This one looked simple.

The Long Goodbye

TIME

The minutes went by on tiptoe, with their fingers to their lips.

The Lady in the Lake

TOUGH GUYS

"Know who I am, cheapie?"

"Your name's Menendez. The boys call you Mendy. You operate on the Strip."

"Yeah? How did I get so big?"

"I wouldn't know. You probably started out as a pimp in a Mexican whorehouse."

The Long Goodbye

"Okay, tough boy. Quite a man, aren't you? You know something? They're all sizes and shapes when they come in here, but they go out the same size— small. And the same shape—bent."

The Long Goodbye

TROUBLE

Terry Lennox made me plenty of trouble. But after all, that's my line of work.

The Long Goodbye

VEGETARIANS

You can't tell a doper well under control from a vegetarian bookkeeper.

The Long Goodbye

VENTURA BOULEVARD

Fast boys in stripped-down Fords shot
in and out of the traffic streams,
missing fenders by a sixteenth of an
inch, but somehow always missing
them. Tired men in dusty coupés and
sedans winced and tightened their
grip on the wheel and ploughed on
north and west towards home and
dinner, an evening with the sports
page, the blatting of the radio, the
whining of their spoiled children and
the gabble of their silly wives. I
drove on past the gaudy neons and the
false fronts behind them, the sleazy
hamburger joints that look like
palaces under the colors.

The Little Sister

WILD FLOWERS

A few locks of dry white hair clung to
his scalp, like wild flowers fighting
for life on a bare rock.

The Big Sleep

On the other side of the road was a
raw clay bank at the edge of which a
few unbeatable wild flowers hung on
like naughty children that won't go
to bed.

Farewell, My Lovely

WOMEN'S CLOTHING

She was wearing a white wool skirt, a
burgundy silk blouse and a black
velvet over-jacket with short sleeves.
Her hair was a hot sunset. She wore a
golden topaz bracelet and topaz
earrings and a topaz dinner ring in

the shape of a shield. Her fingernails
matched her blouse exactly. She
looked as if it would take a couple of
weeks to get her dressed.

The Little Sister

She nodded and got up slowly from
behind the desk. She swished before
me in a tight dress that fitted her
like a mermaid's skin and showed that
she had a good figure if you like them
four sizes bigger below the waist.

Farewell, My Lovely

"Don't make me dress you again. I'm
tired. I appreciate all you're
offering me. It's just more than I
could possibly take."

The Big Sleep

WRITERS

"I'm a writer," Wade said. "I'm supposed to understand what makes people tick. I don't understand one damn thing about anybody."

The Long Goodbye

About the Author

Raymond Thornton Chandler (1888–1959) was the master practitioner of American hard-boiled crime fiction. Although he was born in Chicago, Chandler spent most of his boyhood and youth in England, where he attended Dulwich College and later worked as a freelance journalist for the *Westminster Gazette* and the *Spectator*. During World War I, Chandler served in France with the First Division of the Canadian Expeditionary Force, transferring later to the Royal Flying Corps (later called the RAF). In 1919 he returned to the United States, settling in California, where he eventually became director of a number of independent oil companies. The Depression put an end to his career, and in 1933, at the age of forty-five, he turned to writing fiction, publishing his first stories in *Black Mask*. Chandler's detective stories often starred the brash but honorable Philip Marlowe (introduced in 1939 in his first novel, *The Big Sleep*) and were noted for their literate presentation and dead-on critical eye. Never a prolific writer, Chandler published only two collections of stories and seven novels in his lifetime.

Some of Chandler's novels, like *The Big Sleep*, were made into classic movies that helped define the film noir style. In the last year of his life he was elected president of the Mystery Writers of America. He died in La Jolla, California, on March 26, 1959.

About the Editor

Martin Asher is executive vice president and editor in chief of Vintage/Anchor Books. He lives in Connecticut.

About the Type

The extracts from the books of Raymond Chandler were set in the portentously named typeface Dear John. Created in 2001 by Lloyd Springer, the founder of the TypeArt Foundry in Vancouver, British Columbia, Dear John is one of a generation of fonts that strive for irony, idiosyncrasy, and imperfection, in contrast to the regularity and precision traditionally valued in fonts over the centuries.

Composed by Creative Graphics,
Allentown, Pennsylvania
Printed and bound by
United Book Press,
Baltimore, Maryland
Designed by Peter A. Andersen
and Pamela G. Parker